D0112139

The Octoroon

Dion Boucicault

Copyright © 2017 Okitoks Press

All rights reserved.

ISBN: 1548246603

ISBN-13: 978-1548246600

Table of Contents

ACT I.

Scene I.—*A view of the Plantation Terrebonne, in Louisiana.—A branch of the Mississippi is seen winding through the Estate.—A low built, but extensive Planter's Dwelling, surrounded with a veranda, and raised a few feet from the ground, occupies the L. side.—A table and chairs, R. C.*

GRACE *discovered sitting at breakfast-table with Children.*

Enter SOLON, *from house,* L.

Solon. Yah! you bomn'ble fry—git out—a gen'leman can't pass for you.

Grace. [*Seizing a fly whisk.*] Hee! ha—git out! [*Drives* CHILDREN *away; in escaping they tumble against and trip up* SOLON, *who falls with tray; the* CHILDREN *steal the bananas and rolls that fall about.*]

Enter PETE, R. U. E. [*he is lame*]; *he carries a mop and pail.*

Pete. Hey! laws a massey! why, clar out! drop dat banana! I'll murder this yer crowd, [*He chases* CHILDREN *about; they leap over railing at back. Exit* SOLON, R. U. E.] Dem little niggers is a judgment upon dis generation.

Enter GEORGE, *from house,* L.

George. What's the matter, Pete.

Pete. It's dem black trash, Mas'r George; dis ere property wants claring; dem's getting too numerous round; when I gets time I'll kill some on 'em, sure!

George. They don't seem to be scared by the threat.

3

Pete. Top, you varmin! top till I get enough of you in one place!

George. Were they all born on this estate?

Pete. Guess they nebber was born—dem tings! what, dem?—get away! Born here—dem darkies? What, on Terrebonne! Don't b'lieve it, Mas'r George; dem black tings never was born at all; dey swarmed one mornin' on a sassafras tree in the swamp: I cotched 'em; dey ain't no 'count. Don't b'lieve dey'll turn out niggers when dey're growed; dey'll come out sunthin else.

Grace. Yes, Mas'r George, dey was born here; and old Pete is fonder on 'em dan he is of his fiddle on a Sunday.

Pete. What? dem tings—dem?—getaway [*makes blow at the* CHILDREN.] Born here! dem darkies! What, on Terrebonne? Don't b'lieve it, Mas'r George,—no. One morning dey swarmed on a sassafras tree in de swamp, and I cotched 'em all in a sieve.—dat's how dey come on top of dis yearth—git out, you,—ya, ya! [*Laughs.*]

[*Exit* GRACE, R. U. E.

Enter MRS. PEYTON, from house.

Mrs. P. So, Pete, you are spoiling those children as usual!

Pete. Dat's right, missus! gib it to ole Pete! he's allers in for it. Git away dere! Ya! if dey aint all lighted, like coons, on dat snake fence, just out of shot. Look dar! Ya! ya! Dem debils. Ya!

Mrs. P. Pete, do you hear?

Pete. Git down dar!—I'm arter you!

[*Hobbles off,* R. 1. E.

Mrs. P. You are out early this morning, George.

4

George. I was up before daylight. We got the horses saddled, and galloped down the shell road over the Piney Patch; then coasting the Bayou Lake, we crossed the long swamps, by Paul's Path, and so came home again.

Mrs. P. [*Laughing.*] You seem already familiar with the names of every spot on the estate.

Enter PETE.—*Arranges breakfast, &c.*

George. Just one month ago I quitted Paris. I left that siren city as I would have left a beloved woman.

Mrs. P. No wonder! I dare say you left at least a dozen beloved women there, at the same time.

George. I feel that I departed amid universal and sincere regret. I left my loves and my creditors equally inconsolable.

Mrs. P. George, you are incorrigible. Ah! you remind me so much of your uncle, the judge.

George. Bless his dear old handwriting, it's all I ever saw of him. For ten years his letters came every quarter-day, with a remittance and a word of advice in his formal cavalier style; and then a joke in the postscript, that upset the dignity of the foregoing. Aunt, when he died, two years ago, I read over those letters of his, and if I didn't cry like a baby—

Mrs. P. No, George; say you wept like a man. And so you really kept those foolish letters?

George. Yes; I kept the letters, and squandered the money.

Mrs. P. [*Embracing him.*] Ah! why were you not my son—you are so like my dear husband.

Enter SALEM SCUDDER, R.

Scud. Ain't he! Yes—when I saw him and Miss Zoe galloping through the green sugar crop, and doing ten dollars' worth of damage at every stride, says I, how like his old uncle he do make the dirt fly.

George. O, aunt! what a bright, gay creature she is!

Scud. What, Zoe! Guess that you didn't leave anything female in Europe that can lift an eyelash beside that gal. When she goes along, she just leaves a streak of love behind her. It's a good drink to see her come into the cotton fields—the niggers get fresh on the sight of her. If she ain't worth her weight in sunshine you may take one of my fingers off, and choose which you like.

Mrs. P. She need not keep us waiting breakfast, though. Pete, tell Miss Zoe that we are waiting.

Pete. Yes, missus. Why, Minnie, why don't you run when you hear, you lazy crittur? [*Minnie runs off.*] Dat's de laziest nigger on dis yere property. [*Sits down.*] Don't do nuffin.

Mrs. P. My dear George, you are left in your uncle's will heir to this estate.

George. Subject to your life interest and an annuity to Zoe, is it not so?

Mrs. P. I fear that the property is so involved that the strictest economy will scarcely recover it. My dear husband never kept any accounts, and we scarcely know in what condition the estate really is.

Scad. Yes, we do, ma'am; it's in a darned bad condition. Ten years ago the judge took as overseer a bit of Connecticut hardware called M'Closky. The judge didn't understand accounts—the overseer did. For a year or two all went fine. The judge drew money like Bourbon whiskey from a barrel, and never turned off the tap. But out it flew, free for everybody or anybody to beg, borrow, or steal. So it went, till one day the judge found the tap wouldn't run. He looked in to see what stopped it, and pulled out a big mortgage. "Sign that," says the overseer; "it's only a formality." "All right," says the judge, and away went a thousand acres; so at the end of eight years, Jacob M'Closky, Esquire, finds himself proprietor of the richest half of Terrebonne—

George. But the other half is free.

Scud. No, it ain't; because, just then, what does the judge do, but hire another overseer—a Yankee—a Yankee named Salem Scudder.

Mrs. P. O, no, it was—

Scud. Hold on, now! I'm going to straighten this account clear out. What was this here Scudder? Well, he lived in New York by sittin' with his heels up in front of French's Hotel, and inventin'—

George. Inventing what?

Scud. Improvements—anything, from a stay-lace to a fire-engine. Well, he cut that for the photographing line. He and his apparatus arrived here, took the judge's likeness and his fancy, who made him overseer right off. Well, sir, what does this Scudder do but introduces his inventions and improvements on this estate. His new cotton gins broke down, the steam sugar-mills burst up, until he finished off with his folly what Mr. M'Closky with his knavery began.

Mrs. P. O, Salem! how can you say so? Haven't you worked like a horse?

Scud. No, ma'am, I worked like an ass—an honest one, and that's all. Now, Mr. George, between the two overseers, you and that good old lady have come to the ground; that is the state of things, just as near as I can fix it. [*Zoe sings without,* L.]

George. 'Tis Zoe.

Scud. O, I have not spoiled that anyhow. I can't introduce any darned improvement there. Ain't that a cure for old age; it kinder lifts the heart up, don't it?

Mrs. P. Poor child! what will become of her when I am gone? If you haven't spoiled her, I fear I have. She has had the education of a lady.

George. I have remarked that she is treated by the neighbors with a kind of familiar condescension that annoyed me.

Scud. Don't you know that she is the natural daughter of the judge, your uncle, and that old lady thar just adored anything her husband cared for; and this girl, that another woman would a hated, she loves as if she'd been her own child.

George. Aunt, I am prouder and happier to be your nephew and heir to the ruins of Terrebonne, than I would have been to have had half Louisiana without you.

Enter ZOE, *from house,* L.

Zoe. Am I late? Ah! Mr. Scudder, good morning.

Scud. Thank'ye. I'm from fair to middlin', like a bamboo cane, much the same all the year round.

Zoe. No; like a sugar cane; so dry outside, one would never think there was so much sweetness within.

Scud. Look here; I can't stand that gal! if I stop here, I shall hug her right off. [*Sees* PETE, *who has set his pail down* L. C. *up stage, and goes to sleep on it.*] If that old nigger ain't asleep, I'm blamed. Hillo! [*Kicks pail from under* PETE, *and lets him down.*]

[*Exit,* L. U. E.

Pete. Hi! Debbel's in de pail! Whar's breakfass?

8

Enter SOLON *and* DIDO *with coffee-pot, dishes, &c.,* R. U. E.

Dido. Bless'ee, Missey Zoe, here it be. Dere's a dish of pen-pans—jess taste, Mas'r George—and here's fried bananas; smell 'em, do, sa glosh.

Pete. Hole yer tongue, Dido. Whar's de coffee? [*Pours out.*] If it don't stain de cup, your wicked ole life's in danger, sure! dat right! black as nigger; clar as ice. You may drink dat, Mas'r George. [*Looks off.*] Yah! here's Mas'r Sunnyside, and Missey Dora, jist drov up. Some of you niggers run and hole de hosses; and take dis, Dido. [*Gives her coffee-pot to hold, and hobbles off, followed by* SOLON *and* DIDO, R. U. E.]

Enter SUNNYSIDE *and* DORA, R. U. E.

Sunny. Good day, ma'am. [*Shakes hands with* GEORGE.] I see we are just in time for breakfast. [*Sits,* R.]

Dora. O, none for me; I never eat. [*Sits,* R. C.]

George. [*Aside.*] They do not notice Zoe.—[*Aloud.*] You don't see Zoe, Mr. Sunnyside.

Sunny. Ah! Zoe, girl; are you there?

Dora. Take my shawl, Zoe. [ZOE *helps her.*] What a good creature she is.

Sunny. I dare say, now, that in Europe you have never met any lady more beautiful in person, or more polished in manners, than that girl.

George. You are right, sir; though I shrank from expressing that opinion in her presence, so bluntly.

Sunny. Why so?

9

George. It may be considered offensive.

Sunny. [*Astonished.*] What? I say, Zoe, do you hear that?

Dora. Mr. Peyton is joking.

Mrs. P. [L. C.] My nephew is not acquainted with our customs in Louisiana, but he will soon understand.

George. Never, aunt! I shall never understand how to wound the feelings of any lady; and, if that is the custom here, I shall never acquire it.

Dora. Zoe, my dear, what does he mean?

Zoe. I don't know.

George. Excuse me, I'll light a cigar. [*Goes up.*]

Dora. [*Aside to Zoe.*] Isn't he sweet! O, dear Zoe, is he in love with anybody?

Zoe. How can I tell?

Dora. Ask him, I want to know; don't say I told you to inquire, but find out. Minnie, fan me, it is so nice—and his clothes are French, ain't they?

Zoe. I think so; shall I ask him that too?

Dora. No, dear. I wish he would make love to me. When he speaks to one he does it so easy, so gentle; it isn't bar-room style; love lined with drinks, sighs tinged with tobacco—and they say all the women in Paris were in love with him, which I feel *I* shall be; stop fanning me; what nice boots he wears.

Sunny. [*To* Mrs. Peyton.] Yes, ma'am, I hold a mortgage over Terrebonne; mine's a ninth, and pretty near covers all the property,

10

except the slaves. I believe Mr. M'Closky has a bill of sale on them. O, here he is.

Enter M'CLOSKY, R. U. E.

Sunny. Good morning, Mr. M'Closky.

M'Closky. Good morning, Mr. Sunnyside; Miss Dora, your servant.

Dora. [*Seated,* R. C.] Fan me, Minnie.—[*Aside.*] I don't like that man.

M'Closky. [*Aside,* C.] Insolent as usual.—[*Aloud.*] You begged me to call this morning. I hope I'm not intruding.

Mrs. P. My nephew, Mr. Peyton.

M'Closky. O, how d'ye do, sir? [*Offers hand,* GEORGE *bows coldly,* R. C.] [*aside.*] A puppy, if he brings any of his European airs here we'll fix him.—[*Aloud.*] Zoe, tell Pete to give my mare a feed, will ye?

George. [*Angrily.*] Sir.

M'Closky. Hillo! did I tread on ye?

Mrs. P. What is the matter with George?

Zoe. [*Takes fan from* MINNIE.] Go, Minnie, tell Pete; run!

[*Exit* MINNIE, R.

Mrs. P. Grace, attend to Mr. M'Closky.

M'Closky. A julep, gal, that's my breakfast, and a bit of cheese,

George. [*Aside to* MRS. PEYTON.] How can you ask that vulgar ruffian to your table?

Mrs. P. Hospitality in Europe is a courtesy; here, it is an obligation. We tender food to a stranger, not because he is a gentleman, but because he is hungry.

George. Aunt, I will take my rifle down to the Atchafalaya. Paul has promised me a bear and a deer or two. I see my little Nimrod yonder, with his Indian companion. Excuse me ladies. Ho! Paul! [*Enters house.*]

Paul. [*Outside.*] I'ss, Mas'r George.

Enter PAUL, R. U. E., *with* INDIAN, *who goes up.*

Sunny. It's a shame to allow that young cub to run over the Swamps and woods, hunting and fishing his life away instead of hoeing cane.

Mrs. P. The child was a favorite of the judge, who encouraged his gambols. I couldn't bear to see him put to work.

George. [*Returning with rifle.*] Come, Paul, are you ready?

Paul. I'ss, Mas'r George. O, golly! ain't that a pooty gun.

M'Closky. See here, you imps; if I catch you, and your red skin yonder, gunning in my swamps, I'll give you rats, mind; them vagabonds, when the game's about, shoot my pigs.

[*Exit* GEORGE *into house.*]

Paul. You gib me rattan, Mas'r Clostry, but I guess you take a berry long stick to Wahnotee; ugh, he make bacon of you.

M'Closky. Make bacon of me, you young whelp. Do you mean that I'm a pig? Hold on a bit. [*Seizes whip, and holds* PAUL.]

12

Zoe. O, sir! don't, pray, don't.

M'Closky. [*Slowly lowering his whip,*] Darn you, red skin, I'll pay you off some day, both of ye. [*Returns to table and drinks.*]

Sunny. That Indian is a nuisance. Why don't he return to his nation out West?

M'Closky. He's too fond of thieving and whiskey.

Zoe. No; Wahnotee is a gentle, honest creature, and remains here because he loves that boy with the tenderness of a woman. When Paul was taken down with the swamp fever the Indian sat outside the hut, and neither ate, slept, or spoke for five days, till the child could recognize and call him to his bedside. He who can love so well is honest—don't speak ill of poor Wahnotee.

Mrs. P. Wahnotee, will you go back to your people?

Wahnotee. Sleugh.

Paul. He don't understand; he speaks a mash-up of Indian and Mexican. Wahnotee Patira na sepau assa wigiran.

Wahnotee. Weal Omenee.

Paul. Says he'll go if I'll go with him. He calls me Omenee, the Pigeon, and Miss Zoe is Ninemoosha, the Sweetheart.

Wahnotee. [*Pointing to Zoe.*] Ninemoosha.

Zoe. No, Wahnotee, we can't spare Paul.

Paul. If Omenee remain, Wahnotee will die in Terrebonne. [*During the dialogue* WAHNOTEE *has taken* GEORGE'S *gun.*]

Enter GEORGE, L.

George. Now I'm ready. [GEORGE *tries to regain his gun;* WAHNOTEE *refuses to give it up;* PAUL, *quietly takes it from him and remonstrates with him.*]

Dora. Zoe, he's going; I want him to stay and make love to me that's what I came for to-day.

Mrs. P. George, I can't spare Paul for an hour or two; he must run over to the landing; the steamer from New Orleans passed up the river last night, and if there's a mail they have thrown it ashore.

Sunny. I saw the mail-bags lying in the shed this morning.

Mrs. P. I expect an important letter from Liverpool; away with you, Paul; bring the mail-bags here.

Paul. I'm 'most afraid to take Wahnotee to the shed, there's rum there.

Wahnotee. Rum!

Paul. Come, then, but if I catch you drinkin', O, laws a mussey, you'll get snakes! I'll gib it you! now mind.

[*Exit with* INDIAN, R. U. E.

George. Come, Miss Dora, let me offer you my arm.

Dora. Mr. George, I am afraid, if all we hear is true, you have led a dreadful life in Europe.

George. That's a challenge to begin a description of my feminine adventures.

Dora. You have been in love, then?

George. Two hundred and forty-nine times! Let me relate you the worst cases.

14

Dora. No! no!

George. I'll put the naughty parts in French.

Dora. I won't hear a word! O, you horrible man! go on.

[*Exit* GEORGE *and* DORA *to house.*

M'Closky. Now, ma'am, I'd like a little business, if agreeable. I bring you news; your banker, old Lafouche, of New Orleans, is dead; the executors are winding up his affairs, and have foreclosed on all overdue mortgages, so Terrebonne is for sale. Here's the Picayune [*producing paper*] with the advertisement.

Zoe. Terrebonne for sale!

Mrs. P. Terrebonne for sale, and you, sir, will doubtless become its purchaser.

M'Closky. Well, ma'am, I spose there's no law agin my bidding for it. The more bidders, the better for you. You'll take care, I guess, it don't go too cheap.

Mrs. P. O, sir, I don't value the place for its price, but for the many happy days I've spent here; that landscape, flat and uninteresting though it may be, is full of charm for me; those poor people, born around me, growing up about my heart, have bounded my view of life; and now to lose that homely scene, lose their black, ungainly faces; O, sir, perhaps you should be as old as I am, to feel as I do, when my past life is torn away from me.

M'Closky. I'd be darned glad if somebody would tear my past life away from me. Sorry I can't help you, but the fact is, you're in such an all-fired mess that you couldn't be pulled out without a derrick.

Mrs. P. Yes, there is a hope left yet, and I cling to it. The house of Mason Brothers, of Liverpool, failed some twenty years ago in my husband's debt.

M'Closky. They owed him over fifty thousand dollars.

Mrs. P. I cannot find the entry in my husband's accounts; but you, Mr. M'Closky, can doubtless detect it. Zoe, bring here the judge's old desk; it is in the library.

[*Exit* ZOE *to house.*

M'Closky. You don't expect to recover any of this old debt, do you?

Mrs. P. Yes; the firm has recovered itself, and I received a notice two months ago that some settlement might be anticipated.

Sunny. Why, with principal and interest this debt has been more than doubled in twenty years.

Mrs. P. But it may be years yet before it will be paid off, if ever.

Sunny. If there's a chance of it, there's not a planter round here who wouldn't lend you the whole cash, to keep your name and blood amongst us. Come, cheer up, old friend.

Mrs. P. Ah! Sunnyside, how good you are; so like my poor Peyton.

[*Exit* MRS. PEYTON *and* SUNNYSIDE *to house.*

M'Closky. Curse their old families—they cut me—a bilious, conceited, thin lot of dried up aristocracy. I hate 'em. Just because my grandfather wasn't some broken-down Virginia transplant, or a stingy old Creole, I ain't fit to sit down with the same meat with them. It makes my blood so hot I feel my heart hiss. I'll sweep these Peytons from this section of the country. Their presence keeps alive the reproach against me that I ruined them; yet, if this money should come. Bah! There's no chance of it. Then, if they go, they'll take Zoe—she'll follow them. Darn that girl; she makes me quiver when I think of her; she's took me for all I'm worth.

Enter ZOE *from house,* L., *with the desk.*

O, here, do you know what annuity the old judge left you is worth to-day? Not a picayune.

Zoe. It's surely worth the love that dictated it; here are the papers and accounts. [*Putting it on the table,* R. C.]

M'Closky. Stop, Zoe; come here! How would you like to rule the house of the richest planter on Atchafalaya—eh? or say the word, and I'll buy this old barrack, and you shall be mistress of Terrebonne.

Zoe. O, sir, do not speak so to me!

M'Closky. Why not! look here, these Peytons are bust; cut 'em; I am rich, jine me; I'll set you up grand, and we'll give these first families here our dust, until you'll see their white skins shrivel up with hate and rage; what d'ye say?

Zoe. Let me pass! O, pray, let me go!

M'Closky. What, you won't, won't ye? If young George Peyton was to make you the same offer, you'd jump at it, pretty darned quick, I guess. Come, Zoe, don't be a fool; I'd marry you if I could, but you know I can't; so just say what you want. Here then, I'll put back these Peytons in Terrebonne, and they shall know you done it; yes, they'll have you to thank for saving them from ruin.

Zoe. Do you think they would live here on such terms?

M'Closky, Why not? We'll hire out our slaves, and live on their wages.

Zoe. But I'm not a slave.

M'Closky. No; if you were I'd buy you, if you cost all I'm worth.

Zoe. Let me pass!

M'Closky. Stop.

Enter SCUDDER, R.

Scud. Let her pass.

M'Closky. Eh?

Scud. Let her pass! [*Takes out his knife.*]

[*Exit* ZOE *to house.*

M'Closky. Is that you, Mr. Overseer? [*Examines paper.*]

Scud. Yes, I'm here, somewhere, interferin'.

M'Closky. [*Sitting,* R. C.] A pretty mess you've got this estate in—

Scud. Yes—me and Co.—we done it; but, as you were senior partner in the concern, I reckon you got the big lick.

M'Closky. What d'ye mean.

Scud. Let me proceed by illustration. [*Sits,* R.] Look thar! [*Points with knife off,* R.] D'ye see that tree?—it's called a live oak, and is a native here; beside it grows a creeper; year after year that creeper twines its long arms round and round the tree—sucking the earth dry all about its roots—living on its life—overrunning its branches, until at last the live oak withers and dies out. Do you know what the niggers round here call that sight? they call it the Yankee hugging the Creole. [*Sits.*]

M'Closky. Mr. Scudder, I've listened to a great many of your insinuations, and now I'd like to come to an understanding what they mean. If you want a quarrel—

18

Scudder. No, I'm the skurriest crittur at a fight you ever see; my legs have been too well brought up to stand and see my body abused; I take good care of myself, I can tell you.

M'Closky. Because I heard that you had traduced my character.

Scud. Traduced! Whoever said so lied. I always said you were the darndest thief that ever escaped a white jail to misrepresent the North to the South.

M'Closky. [*Raises hand to back of his neck.*] What!

Scud. Take your hand down—take it down. [M'CLOSKY *lowers his hand.*] Whenever I gets into company like yours, I always start with the advantage on my side.

M'Closky. What d'ye mean?

Scud. I mean that before you could draw that bowie-knife, you wear down your back, I'd cut you into shingles. Keep quiet, and let's talk sense. You wanted to come to an understanding, and I'm coming thar as quick as I can. Now, Jacob M'Closky, you despise me because you think I'm a fool; I despise you because I know you to be a knave. Between us we've ruined these Peytons; you fired the judge, and I finished off the widow. Now, I feel bad about my share in the business. I'd give half the balance of my life to wipe out my part of the work. Many a night I've laid awake and thought how to pull them through, till I've cried like a child over the sum I couldn't do; and you know how darned hard 'tis to make a Yankee cry.

M'Closky. Well, what's that to me?

Scud. Hold on, Jacob, I'm coming to that—I tell ye, I'm such a fool—I can't bear the feeling, it keeps at me like a skin complaint, and if this family is sold up—

M'Closky. What then?

19

Scud. [*Rising.*] I'd cut my throat—or yours—yours I'd prefer.

M'Closky. Would you now? why don't you do it?

Scud. 'Cos I's skeered to try! I never killed a man in my life—and civilization is so strong in me I guess I couldn't do it—I'd like to, though!

M'Closky. And all for the sake of that old woman and that young puppy—eh? No other cause to hate—to envy me—to be jealous of me—eh?

Scud. Jealous! what for?

M'Closky. Ask the color in your face; d'ye think I can't read you, like a book? With your New England hypocrisy, you would persuade yourself it was this family alone you cared for; it ain't— you know it ain't—'tis the "Octoroon;" and you love her as I do; and you hate me because I'm your rival—that's where the tears come from, Salem Scudder, if you ever shed any—that's where the shoe pinches.

Scud. Wal, I do like the gal; she's a—

M'Closky. She's in love with young Peyton; it made me curse, whar it made you cry, as it does now; I see the tears on your cheeks now.

Scud. Look at 'em, Jacob, for they are honest water from the well of truth. I ain't ashamed of it—I do love the gal; but I ain't jealous of you, because I believe the only sincere feeling about you is your love for Zoe, and it does your heart good to have her image thar; but I believe you put it thar to spile. By fair means I don't think you can get her, and don't you try foul with her, 'cause if you do, Jacob, civilization be darned. I'm on you like a painter, and when I'm drawed out I'm pizin.

[*Exit* SCUDDER *to house,* L.

20

M'Closky. Fair or foul, I'll have her—take that home with you! [*Opens desk.*] What's here—judgments? yes, plenty of 'em; bill of costs; account with Citizens' Bank—what's this? "Judgment, 40,000, 'Thibodeaux against Peyton,'"—surely, that is the judgment under which this estate is now advertised for sale— [*takes up paper and examines it*]; yes, "Thibodeaux against Peyton, 1838." Hold on! whew! this is worth taking to—in this desk the judge used to keep one paper I want—this should be it. [*Reads.*] "The free papers of my daughter, Zoe, registered February 4th, 1841." Why, judge, wasn't you lawyer enough to know that while a judgment stood against you it was a lien on your slaves? Zoe is your child by a quadroon slave, and you didn't free her; blood! if this is so, she's mine! this old Liverpool debt—that may cross me—if it only arrive too late—if it don't come by this mail—Hold on! this letter the old lady expects—that's it; let me only head off that letter, and Terrebonne will be sold before they can recover it. That boy and the Indian have gone down to the landing for the post-bags; they'll idle on the way as usual; my mare will take me across the swamp, and before they can reach the shed, I'll have purified them bags—ne'er a letter shall show this mail. Ha, ha!— [*Calls.*] Pete, you old turkey-buzzard, saddle my mare. Then, if I sink every dollar I'm worth in her purchase, I'll own that Octoroon. [*Stands with his hand extended towards the house, and tableau.*]

END OF THE FIRST ACT.

ACT II.

The Wharf—goods, boxes, and bales scattered about—a camera on stand, R.

SCUDDER, R., DORA, L., GEORGE *and* PAUL *discovered;* DORA *being photographed by* SCUDDER, *who is arranging photographic apparatus,* GEORGE *and* PAUL *looking on at back.*

21

Scud. Just turn your face a leetle this way—fix your—let's see—look here.

Dora. So?

Scud. That's right. [*Puts his head under the darkening apron.*] It's such a long time since I did this sort of thing, and this old machine has got so dirty and stiff, I'm afraid it won't operate. That's about right. Now don't stir.

Paul. Ugh! she look as though she war gwine to have a tooth drawed!

Scud. I've got four plates ready, in case we miss the first shot. One of them is prepared with a self-developing liquid that I've invented. I hope it will turn out better than most of my notions. Now fix yourself. Are you ready?

Dora. Ready!

Scud. Fire!—one, two, three. [SCUDDER *takes out watch.*]

Paul. Now it's cooking, laws mussey, I feel it all inside, as if it was at a lottery.

Scud. So! [*Throws down apron.*] That's enough. [*With-draws slide, turns and sees* PAUL.] What! what are you doing there, you young varmint! Ain't you took them bags to the house yet?

Paul. Now, it ain't no use trying to get mad, Mas'r Scudder. I'm gwine! I only come back to find Wahnotee; whar is dat ign'ant Ingiun?

Scud. You'll find him scenting round the rum store, hitched up by the nose.

[*Exit into room,* R.

Paul. [*Calling at door.*] Say, Mas'r Scudder, take me in dat telescope?

Scud. [*Inside room.*] Get out, you cub! clar out!

Paul. You got four of dem dishes ready. Gosh, wouldn't I like to hab myself took! What's de charge, Mas'r Scudder?

[*Runs off,* R. U. E.

Enter SCUDDER, *from room,* R.

Scud. Job had none of them critters on his plantation, else he'd never ha' stood through so many chapters. Well, that has come out clear, ain't it? [*Shows plate.*]

Dora. O, beautiful! Look, Mr. Peyton.

George. [*Looking.*] Yes, very fine!

Scud. The apparatus can't mistake. When I travelled round with this machine, the homely folks used to sing out, "Hillo, mister, this ain't like me!" "Ma'am," says I, "the apparatus can't mistake." "But, mister, that ain't my nose." "Ma'am, your nose drawed it. The machine can't err—you may mistake your phiz but the apparatus don't." "But, sir, it ain't agreeable." "No, ma'am, the truth seldom is."

Enter PETE, L. U. E., *puffing.*

Pete. Mas'r Scudder! Mas'r Scudder!

Scud. Hillo! what are you blowing about like a steamboat with one wheel for?

Pete. You blow, Mas'r Scudder, when I tole you; dere's a man from Noo Aleens just arriv' at de house, and he's stuck up two papers on de gates; "For sale—dis yer property," and a heap of oder tings—

23

and he seen missus, and arter he shown some papers she burst out crying—I yelled; den de corious of little niggers dey set up, den de hull plantation children—de live stock reared up and created a purpiration of lamentation as did de ole heart good to har.

Dora. What's the matter?

Scud. He's come.

Pete. Dass it—I saw'm!

Scud. The sheriff from New Orleans has taken possession—Terrebonne is in the hands of the law.

Enter ZOE, L. U. E.

Zoe. O, Mr. Scudder! Dora! Mr. Peyton! come home—there are strangers in the house.

Dora. Stay, Mr. Peyton; Zoe, a word! [*Leads her forward—aside.*] Zoe, the more I see of George Peyton the better I like him; but he is too modest—that is a very impertinent virtue in a man.

Zoe. I'm no judge, dear.

Dora. Of course not, you little fool; no one ever made love to you, and you can't understand; I mean, that George knows I am an heiress; my fortune would release this estate from debt.

Zoe. O, I see!

Dora. If he would only propose to marry me I would accept him, but he don't know that, and he will go on fooling, in his slow European way, until it is too late.

Zoe. What's to be done?

Dora. You tell him.

Zoe. What? that he isn't to go on fooling in his slow—

Dora. No, you goose! twit him on his silence and abstraction—I'm sure it's plain enough, for he has not spoken two words to me all the day; then joke round the subject, and at last speak out.

Scud. Pete, as you came here, did you pass Paul and the Indian with the letter-bags?

Pete. No, sar; but dem vagabonds neber take de 'specable straight road, dey goes by de swamp.

[*Exit up path,* L. U. E.

Scud. Come, sir!

Dora. [*To* ZOE.] Now's your time.—[*Aloud.*] Mr. Scudder, take us with you—Mr. Peyton is so slow, there's no getting him, on.

[*Exit* DORA *and* SCUDDER, L. U. E.

Zoe. They are gone!—[*Glancing at* GEORGE.] Poor fellow, he has lost all.

George. Poor child! how sad she looks now she has no resource.

Zoe. How shall I ask him to stay?

George. Zoe, will you remain here? I wish to speak to you.

Zoe. [*Aside.*] Well, that saves trouble.

George. By our ruin, you lose all.

Zoe. O, I'm nothing; think of yourself.

George. I can think of nothing but the image that remains face to face with me: so beautiful, so simple, so confiding, that I dare not express the feelings that have grown up so rapidly in my heart.

Zoe. [*Aside.*] He means Dora.

George. If I dared to speak!

Zoe. That's just what you must do, and do it at once, or it will be too late.

George. Has my love been divined?

Zoe. It has been more than suspected.

George. Zoe, listen to me, then. I shall see this estate pass from me without a sigh, for it possesses no charm for me; the wealth I covet is the love of those around me—eyes that are rich in fond looks, lips that breathe endearing words; the only estate I value is the heart of one true woman, and the slaves I'd have are her thoughts.

Zoe. George, George, your words take away my breath!

George. The world, Zoe, the free struggle of minds and hands, if before me; the education bestowed on me by my dear uncle is a noble heritage which no sheriff can seize; with that I can build up a fortune, spread a roof over the heads I love, and place before them the food I have earned; I will work—

Zoe. Work! I thought none but colored people worked.

George. Work, Zoe, is the salt that gives savor to life.

Zoe. Dora said you were slow; if she could hear you now—

George. Zoe, you are young; your mirror must have told you that you are beautiful. Is your heart free?

26

Zoe. Free? of course it is!

George. We have known each other but a few days, but to me those days have been worth all the rest of my life. Zoe, you have suspected the feeling that now commands an utterance—you have seen that I love you.

Zoe. Me! you love me?

George. As my wife,—the sharer of my hopes, my ambitions, and my sorrows; under the shelter of your love I could watch the storms of fortune pass unheeded by.

Zoe. My love! My love? George, you know not what you say. I the sharer of your sorrows—your wife. Do you know what I am?

George. Your birth—I know it. Has not my dear aunt forgotten it—she who had the most right to remember it? You are illegitimate, but love knows no prejudice.

Zoe. [*Aside.*] Alas! he does not know, he does not know! and will despise me, spurn me, loathe me, when he learns who, what, he has so loved.—[*Aloud.*] George, O, forgive me! Yes, I love you—I did not know it until your words showed me what has been in my heart; each of them awoke a new sense, and now I know how unhappy—how very unhappy I am.

George. Zoe, what have I said to wound you?

Zoe. Nothing; but you must learn what I thought you already knew. George, you cannot marry me; the laws forbid it!

George. Forbid it?

Zoe. There is a gulf between us, as wide as your love, as deep as my despair; but, O, tell me, say you will pity me! that you will not throw me from you like a poisoned thing!

George. Zoe, explain yourself—your language fills me with shapeless fears.

Zoe. And what shall I say? I—my mother was—no, no—not her! Why should I refer the blame to her? George, do you see that hand you hold? look at these fingers; do you see the nails are of a bluish tinge?

George. Yes, near the quick there is a faint blue mark.

Zoe. Look in my eyes; is not the same color in the white?

George. It is their beauty.

Zoe. Could you see the roots of my hair you would see the same dark, fatal mark. Do you know what that is?

George. No.

Zoe. That is the ineffaceable curse of Cain. Of the blood that feeds my heart, one drop in eight is black—bright red as the rest may be, that one drop poisons all the flood; those seven bright drops give me love like yours—hope like yours—ambition like yours—Life hung with passions like dew-drops on the morning flowers; but the one black drop gives me despair, for I'm an unclean thing— forbidden by the laws—I'm an Octoroon!

George. Zoe, I love you none the less; this knowledge brings no revolt to my heart, and I can overcome the obstacle.

Zoe. But I cannot.

George. We can leave this country, and go far away where none can know.

Zoe. And our mother, she who from infancy treated me with such fondness, she who, as you said, had most reason to spurn me, can she forget what I am? Will she gladly see you wedded to the child of her husband's slave? No! she would revolt from it, as all but you would; and if I consented to hear the cries of my heart, if I did not crush out my infant love, what would she say to the poor girl on whom she had bestowed so much? No, no!

George. Zoe, must we immolate our lives on her prejudice?

Zoe. Yes, for I'd rather be black than ungrateful! Ah, George, our race has at least one virtue—it knows how to suffer!

George. Each word you utter makes my love sink deeper into my heart.

Zoe. And I remained here to induce you to offer that heart to Dora!

George. If you bid me do so I will obey you—

Zoe. No, no! if you cannot be mine, O, let me not blush when I think of you.

George. Dearest Zoe!

[*Exit* George *and* Zoe, L. U. E.

As they exit, M'Closky *rises from behind rock, R., and looks after them.*

M'Olosky. She loves him! I felt it—and how she can love! [*Advances.*] That one black drop of blood burns in her veins and lights up her heart like a foggy sun. O, how I lapped up her words, like a thirsty bloodhound! I'll have her, if it costs me my life! Yonder the boy still lurks with those mail-bags; the devil still keeps him here to tempt me, darn his yellow skin. I arrived just too late, he had grabbed the prize as I came up. Hillo! he's coming this way, fighting with his Injiun. [*Conceals himself.*]

Enter Paul, *wrestling with* Wahnotee, R. 3. E.

Paul. It ain't no use now; you got to gib it up!

Wahno. Ugh!

Paul. It won't do! You got dat bottle of rum hid under your blanket—gib it up now, you—Yar! [*Wrenches it from him.*] You nasty, lying Injiun! It's no use you putting on airs; I ain't gwine to sit up wid you all night and you drunk. Hillo! war's de crowd gone? And dar's de 'paratus—O, gosh, if I could take a likeness ob dis child! Uh—uh, let's have a peep. [*Looks through camera*] O, golly! yar, you Wahnotee! you stan' dar, I see you Ta demine usti. [*Goes R., and looks at* WAHNOTEE, L., *through the camera;* WAHNOTEE *springs back with an expression of alarm.*]

Wahno. No tue Wahnotee.

Paul. Ha, ha! he tinks it's a gun. You ign'ant Injiun, it can't hurt you! Stop, here's dem dishes—plates—dat's what he call 'em, all fix: I see Mas'r Scudder do it often—tink I can take likeness—stay dere, Wahnotee.

Wahno. No, carabine tue.

Paul. I must operate and take my own likeness too—how debbel I do dat? Can't be ober dar an' here too—I ain't twins. Ugh' ach! 'Top; you look, you Wahnotee; you see dis rag, eh? Well when I say go, den lift dis rag like dis, see! den run to dat pine tree up dar [*points,* L. U. E.] and back agin, and den pull down de rag so, d'ye see?

Wahno. Hugh!

Paul. Den you hab glass ob rum.

Wahno. Rum!

Paul. Dat wakes him up. Coute Wahnotee in omenee dit go Wahnotee, poina la fa, comb a pine tree, la revieut sala, la fa.

Wahno. Fire-water!

Paul. Yes, den a glass ob fire-water; now den. [*Throws mail bags down and sits on them*, L. C.] Pret, now den go. [WAHNOTEE *raises apron and runs off*, L. U. E. PAUL *sits for his picture—*M'CLOSKY *appears from* R. U. E.]

M'Closky. Where are they? Ah. yonder goes the Indian!

Paul. De time he gone just 'bout enough to cook dat dish plate.

M'Closky. Yonder is the boy—now is my time! What's he doing; is he asleep? [*Advances.*] He is sitting on on my prize! darn his carcass! I'll clear him off there—he'll never know what stunned him. [*Takes Indian's tomahawk and steals to* PAUL.]

Paul. Dam dat Injiun! is dat him creeping dar? I daren't move fear to spile myself. [M'CLOSKY *strikes him on the head—he falls dead.*]

M'Closky. Hooraw! the bags are mine—now for it!—[*Opens mail-bags.*] What's here? Sunnyside, Pointdexter, Jackson, Peyton; here it is—the Liverpool post-mark, sure enough!—[*Opens letter—reads.*] "Madam, we are instructed by the firm of Mason and Co., to inform you that a dividend of forty per cent, is payable on the 1st proximo, this amount in consideration of position, they send herewith, and you will find enclosed by draft to your order, on the Bank of Louisiana, which please acknowledge—the balance will be paid in full, with interest, in three, six, and nine months—your drafts on Mason Brothers at those dates will be accepted by La Palisse and Compagnie, N. O., so that you may command immediate use of the whole amount at once, if required. Yours, &c, James Brown." What a find! this infernal letter would have saved all. [*During the reading of letter he remains nearly motionless under the focus of the camera.*] But now I guess it will arrive too late—these darned U. S. mails are to blame. The injiun! he must not see me.

[*Exit rapidly*, L.

31

[WAHNOTEE *runs on, pulls down apron—sees* PAUL, *lying on ground— speaks to him—thinks he's shamming sleep—gesticulates and jabbers— goes to him—moves him with feet, then kneels down to rouse him—to his horror finds him dead—expresses great grief—raises his eyes— they fall upon the camera—rises with savage growl, seizes tomahawk and smashes camera to pieces, then goes to* PAUL—*expresses grief, sorrow, and fondness, and takes him in his arms to carry him away.— Tableau.*]

END OF THE SECOND ACT.

ACT III.

*A Room in **Mrs. P**eyton's house; entrances,* R. U. E. *and* L. U. E.— *An Auction Bill stuck up,* L.—*chairs,* C., *and tables,* R. and L.

SOLON *and* GRACE *discovered.*

Pete. [*Outside,* R. U. E.] Dis way—dis way.

Enter PETE, POINTDEXTER, JACKSON, LAFOUCHE, *and* CAILLOU, R. U. E.

Pete. Dis way, gen'l'men; now Solon—Grace—dey's hot and tirsty—sangaree, brandy, rum.

Jackson. Well, what d'ye say, Lafouche—d'ye smile?

Enter THIBODEAUX *and* SUNNYSIDE, R. U. E.

Thibo. I hope we don't intrude on the family.

Pete. You see dat hole in dar, sar. [R. U. E.] I was raised on dis yar plantation—neber see no door in it—always open, sar, for stranger to walk in.

Sunny. And for substance to walk out.

Enter RATTS, R. U. E.

Ratts. Fine southern style that, eh!

Lafouche. [*Reading bill.*] "A fine, well-built old family mansion, replete with every comfort."

Ratts. There's one name on the list of slaves scratched, I see.

Lafouche. Yes; No. 49, Paul, a quadroon boy, aged thirteen.

Sunny. He's missing.

Point. Run away, I suppose.

Pete. [*Indignantly.*] No, sar; nigger nebber cut stick on Terrebonne; dat boy's dead, sure.

Ratts. What, Picayune Paul, as we called, him, that used to come aboard my boat?—poor little darkey, I Hope not; many a picayune he picked up for his dance and nigger-songs, and he supplied our table with fish and game from the Bayous.

Pete. Nebber supply no more, sar—nebber dance again. Mas'r Ratts, you hard him sing about de place where de good niggers go, de last time.

Ratts. Well!

Pete. Well, he gone dar hisself; why, I tink so—'cause we missed Paul for some days, but nebber tout nothin' till one night dat Injiun Wahnotee suddenly stood right dar 'mongst us—was in his war paint, and mighty cold and grave—he sit down by de fire. "Whar's Paul?" I say—he smoke and smoke, but nebber look out ob de fire; well knowing dem critters, I wait a long time—den he say, "Wahnotee, great chief;" den I say nothing—smoke anoder time—last, rising to go, he turn round at door, and say berry low—O, like a woman's voice, he say, "Omenee Pangeuk,"—dat is, Paul is dead—nebber see him since.

Ratts. That red-skin killed him.

Sunny. So we believe; and so mad are the folks around, if they catch the red-skin they'll lynch him sure.

Ratts. Lynch him! Darn his copper carcass, I've got a set of Irish deck-hands aboard that just loved that child; and after I tell them this, let them get a sight of the red-skin, I believe they would eat him, tomahawk and all. Poor little Paul!

Thibo. What was he worth?

Ratts. Well, near on five hundred dollars.

Pete. [*Scandalized.*] What, sar! You p'tend to be sorry for Paul, and prize him like dat. Five hundred dollars!—[*To* THIBODEAUX.] Tousand dollars, Massa Thibodeaux.

Enter SCUDDER, L. U. E.

Scud. Gentlemen, the sale takes place at three. Good morning, Colonel. It's near that now, and there's still the sugar-houses to be inspected. Good day, Mr. Thibodeaux—shall we drive down that way? Mr. Lafouche, why, how do you do, sir? you're looking well.

Lafouche. Sorry I can't return the compliment.

Ratts. Salem's looking a kinder hollowed out.

Scud. What, Mr. Ratts, are you going to invest in swamps?

Ratts. No: I want a nigger.

Scud. Hush.

Pete. [R.] Eh! wass dat?

Scud. Mr. Sunnyside, I can't do this job of showin' round the folks; my stomach goes agin it. I want Pete here a minute.

Sunny. I'll accompany them certainly.

Scud. [*Eagerly.*] Will ye? Thank ye; thank ye.

Sunny. We must excuse Scudder, friends. I'll see you round the estate.

Enter GEORGE *and* MRS. PEYTON, L. U. E.

Lafouche. Good morning, Mrs. Peyton. [*All salute.*]

Sunny. This way, gentlemen.

Ratts. [*Aside to Sunnyside.*] I say, I'd like to say summit soft to the old woman; perhaps it wouldn't go well, would it?

Thibo. No; leave it alone.

Ratts. Darn it, when I see a woman in trouble, I feel like selling the skin off my back.

[*Exit* THIBODEAUX, SUNNYSIDE, RATTS, POINTDEXTER, GRACE, JACKSON, LAFOUCHE, CAILLOU, SOLON, R. U. E.

Scud. [*Aside to Pete.*] Go outside, there; listen to what you hear, then go down to the quarters and tell the boys, for I can't do it. O, get out.

Pete. He said I want a nigger. Laws, mussey! What am goin' to cum ob us!

[*Exit slowly, as if concealing himself,* R. U. E.

George. [C.] My dear aunt, why do you not move from this painful scene? Go with Dora to Sunnyside.

Mrs. P. [R.] No, George; your uncle said to me with his dying breath, "Nellie, never leave Terrebonne," and I never will leave it, till the law compels me.

Scud. [L.] Mr. George, I'm going to say somethin' that has been chokin' me for some time. I know you'll excuse it. Thar's Miss Dora—that girl's in love with you; yes, sir, her eyes are startin' out of her head with it; now her fortune would redeem a good part of this estate.

Mrs. P. Why, George, I never suspected this!

George. I did, aunt, I confess, but—

Mrs. P. And you hesitated from motives of delicacy?

Scud. No, ma'am; here's the plan of it. Mr. George is in love with Zoe.

George. Scudder!

Mrs. P. George!

Scud. Hold on now! things have got so jammed in on top of us, we ain't got time to put kid gloves on to handle them. He loves Zoe, and has found out that she loves him. [*Sighing.*] Well, that's all right; but as he can't marry her, and as Miss Dora would jump at him—

Mrs. P. Why didn't you mention this before?

Scud. Why, because I love Zoe, too, and I couldn't take that young feller from her; and she's jist living on the sight of him, as I saw her do; and they so happy in spite of this yer misery around them, and they reproachin' themselves with not feeling as they ought. I've seen it, I tell you; and darn it, ma'am, can't you see that's what's been a hollowing me out so—I beg your pardon.

Mrs. P. O, George,—my son, let me call you,—I do not speak for my own sake, nor for the loss of the estate, but for the poor people here; they will be sold, divided, and taken away—they have been born here. Heaven has denied me children; so all the strings of my heart have grown around and amongst them, like the fibres and roots of an old tree in its native earth. O, let all go, but save them! With them around us, if we have not wealth, we shall at least have the home that they alone can make—

George. My dear mother—Mr. Scudder—you teach me what I ought to do; if Miss Sunnyside will accept me as I am, Terrebonne shall be saved; I will sell myself, but the slaves shall be protected.

Mrs. P. Sell yourself, George! Is not Dora worth any man's—

Scud. Don't say that, ma'am; don't say that to a man that loves another gal. He's going to do an heroic act; don't spile it.

Mrs. P. But Zoe is only an Octoroon.

Scud. She's won this race agin the white, anyhow; it's too late now to start her pedigree.

Enter DORA, L. U. E.

Scud. [*Seeing* DORA.] Come, Mrs. Peyton, take my arm. Hush! here's the other one; she's a little too thoroughbred—too much of the greyhound; but the heart's there, I believe.

[*Exit* SCUDDER *and* MRS. PEYTON, R. U. E.

Dora. Poor Mrs. Peyton.

George. Miss Sunnyside, permit me a word; a feeling of delicacy has suspended upon my lips an avowal, which—

Dora. [*Aside.*] O, dear, has he suddenly come to his senses?

Enter ZOE, L. U. E., *she stops at back.*

George. In a word, I have seen and admired you!

Dora. [*Aside.*] He has a strange way of showing it. European, I suppose.

George. If you would pardon the abruptness of the question, I would ask you, Do you think the sincere devotion of my life to make yours happy would succeed?

Dora. [*Aside.*] Well, he has the oddest way of making love.

George. You are silent?

Dora. Mr. Peyton, I presume you have hesitated to make this avowal because you feared, in the present condition of affairs here, your object might be misconstrued, and that your attention was rather to my fortune than myself. [*A pause.*] Why don't he speak?—I mean, you feared I might not give you credit for sincere and pure feelings. Well, you wrong me. I don't think you capable of anything else than—

George. No, I hesitated because an attachment I had formed before I had the pleasure of seeing you had not altogether died out.

Dora. [*Smiling.*] Some of those sirens of Paris, I presume, [*Pause.*] I shall endeavor not to be jealous of the past; perhaps I have no right to be. [*Pause.*] But now that vagrant love is—eh? faded—is it not? Why don't you speak, sir?

George. Because, Miss Sunnyside, I have not learned to lie.

Dora. Good gracious—who wants you to?

George. I do, but I can't do it. No, the love I speak of is not such as you suppose,—it is a passion that has grown up here since I arrived; but it is a hopeless, mad, wild feeling, that must perish.

Dora. Here! since you arrived! Impossible; you have seen no one; whom can you mean?

Zoe. [*Advancing,* C.] Me.

George. [L.] Zoe!

Dora. [R.] You!

Zoe. Forgive him, Dora; for he knew no better until I told him. Dora, you are right. He is incapable of any but sincere and pure feelings—so are you. He loves me—what of that? You know you can't be jealous of a poor creature like me. If he caught the fever, were stung by a snake, or possessed of any other poisonous or unclean thing, you could pity, tend, love him through it, and for your gentle care he would love you in return. Well, is he not thus afflicted now? I am his love—he loves an Octoroon.

George. O, Zoe, you break my heart!

Dora. At college they said I was a fool—I must be. At New Orleans, they said, "She's pretty, very pretty, but no brains." I'm afraid they must be right; I can't understand a word of all this.

Zoe. Dear Dora, try to understand it with your heart. You love George; you love him dearly; I know it: and you deserve to be loved by him. He will love you—he must. His love for me will pass away—it shall. You heard him say it was hopeless. O, forgive him and me!

39

Dora. [*Weeping.*] O, why did he speak to me at all then? You've made me cry, then, and I hate you both!

[*Exit* L., *through room.*

Enter MRS. PEYTON *and* SCUDDER, M'CLOSKY *and* POINTDEXTER, R.

M'Closky. [C.] I'm sorry to intrude, but the business I came upon will excuse me.

Mrs. Pey. Here is my nephew, sir.

Zoe. Perhaps I had better go.

M'Closky. Wal, as it consarns you, perhaps you better had.

Scud. Consarns Zoe?

M'Closky. I don't know; she may as well hear the hull of it. Go on, Colonel—Colonel Pointdexter, ma'am—the mortgagee, auctioneer, and general agent.

Point. [R. C.] Pardon me, madam, but do you know these papers? [*Hands papers to* MRS. PEYTON.]

Mrs. Pey. [*Takes them.*] Yes, sir; they were the free papers of the girl Zoe; but they were in my husband's secretary. How came they in your possession?

M'Closky. I—I found them.

George. And you purloined them?

M'Closky. Hold on, you'll see. Go on, Colonel.

Point. The list of your slaves is incomplete—it wants one.

Scud. The boy Paul—we know it.

Point. No, sir; you have omitted the Octoroon girl, Zoe.

[*Together.*] *Mrs. Pey.* Zoe!

Zoe. Me!

Point. At the time the judge executed those free papers to his infant slave, a judgment stood recorded against him; while that was on record he had no right to make away with his property. That judgment still exists; under it and others this estate is sold to-day. Those free papers ain't worth the sand that's on 'em.

Mrs. Pey. Zoe a slave! It is impossible!

Point. It is certain, madam; the judge was negligent, and doubtless forgot this small formality.

Scud. But the creditors will not claim the gal?

M'Closky. Excuse me; one of the principal mortgagees has made the demand.

[*Exit* M'CLOSKY *and* POINTDEXTER, R. U. E.

Scud. Hold on yere, George Peyton; you sit down there. You're trembling so, you'll fall down directly. This blow has staggered me some.

Mrs. Pey. O, Zoe, my child! don't think too hardly of your poor father.

Zoe. I shall do so if you weep. See, I'm calm.

Scud. Calm as a tombstone, and with about as much life. I see it in your face.

George. It cannot be! It shall not be!

Scud. Hold your tongue—it must. Be calm—darn the things; the proceeds of this sale won't cover the debts of the estate. Consarn those Liverpool English fellers, why couldn't they send something by the last mail? Even a letter, promising something—such is the feeling round amongst the planters. Darn me, if I couldn't raise thirty thousand on the envelope alone, and ten thousand more on the post-mark.

George. Zoe, they shall not take you from us while I live.

Scud. Don't be a fool; they'd kill you, and then take her, just as soon as—stop; Old Sunnyside, he'll buy her! that'll save her.

Zoe. No, it won't; we have confessed to Dora that we love each other. How can she then ask her father to free me?

Scud. What in thunder made you do that?

Zoe. Because it was the truth; and I had rather be a slave with a free soul, than remain free with a slavish, deceitful heart. My father gives me freedom—at least he thought so. May Heaven bless him for the thought, bless him for the happiness he spread around my life. You say the proceeds of the sale will not cover his debts. Let me be sold then, that I may free his name. I give him back the liberty he bestowed upon me; for I can never repay him the love he bore his poor Octoroon child, on whose breast his last sigh was drawn, into whose eyes he looked with the last gaze of affection.

Mrs. Pey. O, my husband! I thank Heaven you have not lived to see this day.

Zoe. George, leave me! I would be alone a little while.

George. Zoe! [*Turns away overpowered.*]

Zoe. Do not weep, George. Dear George, you now see what a miserable thing I am.

George. Zoe!

Scud. I wish they could sell me! I brought half this ruin on this family, with my all-fired improvements. I deserve to be a nigger this day—I feel like one, inside.

[*Exit* SCUDDER, L. U. E.

Zoe. Go now, George—leave me—take her with you. [*Exit* MRS. PEYTON *and* GEORGE, L. U. E.] A slave! a slave! Is this a dream—for my brain reels with the blow? He said so. What! then I shall be sold!—sold! and my master—O! [*falls on her knees, with her face in her hands*] no—no master, but one. George—George—hush—they come! save me! No, [*looks off,* R.] 'tis Pete and the servants—they come this way. [*Enters inner room,* R. U. E.]

Enter PETE, GRACE, MINNIE, SOLON, DIDO, *and all* NIGGERS, R. U. E.

Pete. Cum yer now—stand round, cause I've got to talk to you darkies—keep dem chil'n quiet—don't make no noise, de missus up dar har us.

Solon. Go on, Pete.

Pete. Gen'l'men, my colored frens and ladies, dar's mighty bad news gone round. Dis yer prop'ty to be sold—old Terrebonne—whar we all been raised, is gwine—dey's gwine to tak it away—can't stop here no how.

Omnes. O-o!—O-o!

Pete. Hold quiet, you trash o' niggers! tink anybody wants you to cry? Who's you to set up screching?—be quiet! But dis ain't all. Now, my culled brethren, gird up your lines, and listen—hold on

43

yer bref—it's a comin. We tought dat de niggers would belong to de ole missus, and if she lost Terrebonne, we must live dere allers, and we would hire out, and bring our wages to ole Missus Peyton.

Omnes. Ya! ya! Well—

Pete. Hush! I tell ye, 't'ain't so—we can't do it—we've got to be sold—

Omnes. Sold!

Pete. Will you hush? she will har you. Yes! I listen dar jess now—dar was ole lady cryin'—Mas'r George—ah! you seen dem big tears in his eyes. O, Mas'r Scudder, he didn't cry zackly; both ob his eyes and cheek look like de bad Bayou in low season—so dry dat I cry for him. [*Raising his voice.*] Den say de missus, "'Tain't for de land I keer, but for dem poor niggars—dey'll be sold—dat wot stagger me." "No," say Mas'r George, "I'd rather sell myself fuss; but dey shan't suffer, nohow,—I see 'em dam fuss."

Omnes. O, bless um! Bless Mas'r George.

Pete. Hole yer tongues. Yes, for you, for me, for dem little ones, dem folks cried. Now, den, if Grace dere wid her chil'n were all sold, she'll begin screechin' like a cat. She didn't mind how kind old judge was to her; and Solon, too, he'll holler, and break de ole lady's heart.

Grace. No, Pete; no, I won't. I'll bear it.

Pete. I don't tink you will any more, but dis here will; 'cause de family spile Dido, dey has. She nebber was 'worth much 'a dat nigger.

Dido. How dar you say dat, you black nigger, you? I fetch as much as any odder cook in Louisiana.

44

Pete. What's de use of your takin' it kind, and comfortin' de missus heart, if Minnie dere, and Louise, and Marie, and Julie is to spile it?

Minnie. We won't, Pete; we won't.

Pete. [*To the men.*] Dar, do ye hear dat, ye mis'able darkies, dem gals is worth a boat load of kinder men dem is. Cum, for de pride of de family, let every darky look his best for the judge's sake—dat ole man so good to us, and dat ole woman—so dem strangers from New Orleans shall say, Dem's happy darkies, dem's a fine set of niggars; every one say when he's sold, "Lor' bless dis yer family I'm gwine out of, and send me as good a home."

Omnes. We'll do it, Pete; we'll do it.

Pete. Hush! hark! I tell ye dar's somebody in dar. Who is it?

Grace. It's Missy Zoe. See! see!

Pete. Come along; she har what we say, and she's cryin' for us. None o' ye ign'rant niggars could cry for yerselves like dat. Come here quite; now quite.

[*Exit* PETE *and all the* NEGROES, *slowly,* R. U. E.

Enter ZOE [*supposed to have overheard the last scene*], L. U. E.

Zoe. O! must I learn from these poor wretches how much I owed, how I ought to pay the debt? Have I slept upon the benefits I received, and never saw, never felt, never knew that I was forgetful and ungrateful? O, my father! my dear, dear father! forgive your poor child. You made her life too happy, and now these tears will be. Let me hide them till I teach my heart. O, my—my heart!

[*Exit, with a low, wailing, suffocating cry,* L. U. E.

Enter M'CLOSKY, LAFOUCHE, JACKSON, SUNNYSLDE, *and*
POINTDEXTER, R. U. E.

Point. [*Looking at watch.*] Come, the hour is past. I think we may
begin business. Where is Mr. Scudder? Jackson, I want to get to
Ophelensis to-night.

Enter DORA, R.

Dora. Father, come here.

Sunny. Why, Dora, what's the matter? Your eyes are red.

Dora. Are they? thank you. I don't care, they were blue this
morning, but it don't signify now.

Sunny. My darling! who has been teasing you?

Dora. Never mind. I want you to buy Terrebonne.

Sunny. Buy Terrebonne! What for?

Dora. No matter—buy it!

Sunny. It will cost me all I'm worth. This is folly, Dora.

Dora. Is my plantation at Comptableau worth this?

Sunny. Nearly—perhaps.

Dora. Sell it, then, and buy this.

Sunny. Are you mad, my love?

Dora. Do you want me to stop here and bid for it?

Sunny. Good gracious! no.

46

Dora. Then I'll do it, if you don't.

Sunny. I will! I will! But for Heaven's sake go—here comes the crowd. [*Exit* DORA, L. U. E.] What on earth does that child mean or want?

Enter SCUDDER, GEORGE, RATTS, CAILLOU, PETE, GRACE, MINNIE, *and all the* NEGROES. *A large table is in the C., at back.* POINTDEXTER *mounts the table with his hammer, his Clerk sits at his feet. The* NEGRO *mounts the table from behind C. The Company sit.*

Point. Now, gentlemen, we shall proceed to business. It ain't necessary for me to dilate, describe, or enumerate; Terrebonne is known to you as one of the richest bits of sile in Louisiana, and its condition reflects credit on them as had to keep it. I'll trouble you for that piece of baccy, Judge—thank you—so, gentlemen, as life is short, we'll start right off. The first lot on here is the estate in block, with its sugar-houses, stock, machines, implements, good dwelling-houses and furniture. If there is no bid for the estate and stuff, we'll sell it in smaller lots. Come, Mr. Thibodeaux, a man has a chance once in his life—here's yours.

Thib. Go on. What's the reserve bid?

Point. The first mortgagee bids forty thousand dollars.

Thib. Forty-five thousand.

Sunny. Fifty thousand.

Point. When you have done joking, gentlemen, you'll say one hundred and twenty thousand. It carried that easy on mortgage.

Lafouche. [R.] Then why don't you buy it yourself, Colonel?

Point. I'm waiting on your fifty thousand bid.

Caillou. Eighty thousand.

Point. Don't be afraid; it ain't going for that, Judge.

Sunny. [L.] Ninety thousand.

Point. We're getting on.

Thib. One hundred—

Point. One hundred thousand bid for this mag—

Caillou. One hundred and ten thousand—

Point. Good again—one hundred and—

Sunny. Twenty.

Point. And twenty thousand bid. Squire Sunnyside is going to sell this at fifty thousand advance to-morrow.—[*Looks round.*] Where's that man from Mobile that wanted to give one hundred and eighty thousand?

Thib. I guess he ain't left home yet, Colonel.

Point. I shall knock it down to the Squire—going—gone—for one hundred and twenty thousand dollars. [*Raises hammer.*] Judge, you can raise the hull on mortgage—going for half its value. [*Knocks.*] Squire Sunnyside, you've got a pretty bit o' land, Squire. Hillo, darkey, hand me a smash dar.

Sunny. I got more than I can work now.

Point. Then buy the hands along with the property. Now, gentlemen, I'm proud to submit to you the finest lot of field hands and house servants that was ever offered for competition; they speak for themselves, and do credit to their owners.—[*Reads.*] "No. 1, Solon, a guess boy, and good waiter."

Pete. [R. C.] That's my son—buy him, Mas'r Ratts; he's sure to sarve you well.

Point. Hold your tongue!

Ratts. [L.] Let the old darkey alone—eight hundred for that boy.

Caillou. Nine.

Ratts. A thousand.

Solon. Thank you, Mas'r Ratts: I die for you, sar; hold up for me, sar.

Ratts. Look here, the boy knows and likes me, Judge; let him come my way?

Caillou. Go on—I'm dumb.

Point. One thousand bid. [*Knocks.*] He's yours, Captain Ratts, Magnolia steamer. [*Solon goes down and stands behind Ratts.*] "No. 2, the yellow girl Grace, with two children—Saul, aged four, and Victoria five." [*They get on table.*]

Scud. That's Solon's wife and children, Judge.

Grace. [*To* RATTS.] Buy me, Mas'r Ratts, do buy me, sar?

Ratts. What in thunder should I do with you and those devils on board my boat?

Grace. Wash, sar—cook, sar—anyting.

Ratts. Eight hundred agin, then—I'll go it.

Jackson. Nine.

Ratts. I'm broke, Solon—I can't stop the Judge.

Thib. What's the matter, Ratts? I'll lend you all you want. Go it, if you're a mind to.

Ratts. Eleven.

Jackson. Twelve.

Sunny. O, O!

Scud. [*To Jackson.*] Judge, my friend. The Judge is a little deaf. Hello! [*Speaking in his ear-trumpet.*] This gal and them children belong to that boy Solon there. You're bidding to separate them, Judge.

Jackson. The devil I am! [*Rises.*] I'll take back my bid, Colonel.

Point. All right, Judge; I thought there was a mistake. I must keep you, Captain, to the eleven hundred.

Ratts. Go it.

Point. Eleven hundred—going—going—sold! "No. 3, Pete, a house servant."

Pete. Dat's me—yer, I'm comin'—stand around dar. [*Tumbles upon the table.*]

Point. Aged seventy-two.

Pete. What's dat? A mistake, sar—forty-six.

Point. Lame.

Pete. But don't mount to nuffin—kin work cannel. Come, Judge, pick up. Now's your time, sar.

Jackson. One hundred dollars.

Pete. What, sar? me! for me—look ye here! [*Dances.*]

George. Five hundred.

Pete. Mas'r George—ah, no, sar—don't buy me—keep your money for some udder dat is to be sold. I ain't no count, sar.

Point. Five hundred bid—it's a good price. [*Knocks.*] He's yours, Mr. George Peyton. [*Pete goes down.*] "No. 4, the Octoroon girl, Zoe."

Enter ZOE, *L. U. E., very pale, and stands on table.*—M'CLOSKY *hitherto has taken no interest in the sale, now turns his chair.*

Sunny. [*Rising.*] Gentlemen, we are all acquainted with the circumstances of this girl's position, and I feel sure that no one here will oppose the family who desires to redeem the child of our esteemed and noble friend, the late Judge Peyton.

Omnes. Hear! bravo! hear!

Point. While the proceeds of this sale promises to realize less than the debts upon it, it is my duty to prevent any collusion for the depreciation of the property.

Ratts. Darn ye! You're a man as well as an auctioneer, ain't ye?

Point. What is offered for this slave?

Sunny. One thousand dollars.

M'Closky. Two thousand.

Sunny. Three thousand.

M'Closky. Five thousand.

George. [R.] Demon!

Sunny. I bid seven thousand, which is the last dollar this family possesses.

M'Closky. Eight.

Thibo. Nine.

Omnes. Bravo!

M'Closky. Ten. It's no use, Squire.

Scud. Jacob M'Closky, you shan't have that girl. Now, take care what you do. Twelve thousand.

M'Closky. Shan't I! Fifteen thousand. Beat that any of ye.

Point. Fifteen thousand bid for the Octoroon.

Enter DORA, L. U. E.

Dora. Twenty thousand.

Omnes. Bravo!

M'Closky. Twenty-five thousand.

Omnes. [*Groan.*] O! O!

George. [L.] Yelping hound—take that. [*Rushes on* M'CLOSKY— M'CLOSKY *draws his knife.*]

Scud. [*Darts between them.*] Hold on, George Peyton—stand back. This is your own house; we are under your uncle's roof; recollect yourself. And, strangers, ain't we forgetting there's a lady present. [*The knives disappear.*] If we can't behave like Christians, let's try and act like gentlemen. Go on, Colonel.

Lafouche. He didn't ought to bid against a lady.

M'Closky. O, that's it, is it? Then I'd like to hire a lady to go to auction and buy my hands.

Point. Gentlemen, I believe none of us have two feelings about the conduct of that man; but he has the law on his side—we may regret, but we must respect it. Mr. M'Closky has bid twenty-five thousand dollars for the Octoroon. Is there any other bid? For the first time, twenty-five thousand—last time! [*Brings hammer down.*] To Jacob M'Closky, the Octoroon girl, Zoe, twenty-five thousand dollars. [*Tableaux.*]

END OF ACT THIRD.

Act IV

SCENE.—*The Wharf, The Steamer "Magnolia" alongside,* L.; *a bluff rock,* R. U. E.

RATTS *discovered, superintending the loading of ship. Enter* LAFOUCHE *and* JACKSON, L.

Jackson. How long before we start, captain?

Raits. Just as soon as we put this cotton on board.

Enter PETE, *with lantern, and* SCUDDER, *with note book,* R.

Scud. One hundred and forty-nine bales. Can you take any more?

Ratts. Not a bale. I've got engaged eight hundred bales at the next landing, and one hundred hogsheads of sugar at Patten's Slide—that'll take my guards under—hurry up thar.

Voice. [*Outside.*] Wood's aboard.

Ratts. All aboard then.

Enter M'CLOSKY, R.

Scud. Sign that receipt, captain, and save me going up to the clerk.

M'Closky. See here—there's a small freight of turpentine in the fore hold there, and one of the barrels leaks; a spark from your engines might set the ship on fire, and you'd go with it.

Ratts. You be darned! Go and try it, if you've a mind to.

Lafouche. Captain, you've loaded up here until the boat is sunk so deep in the mud she won't float.

Ratts. [*Calls off.*] Wood up thar, you Polio—hang on to the safety valve—guess she'll crawl off on her paddles. [*Shouts heard,* R.]

Jackson. What's the matter?

Enter SOLON, R.

Solon. We got him!

Scud. Who?

Solon. The Injiun!

Scud. Wahnotee? Where is he? D'ye call running away from a fellow catching him?

Ratts. Here he comes.

Omnes. Where? Where?

Enter WAHNOTEE, R.; *they are all about to rush on him.*

Scud. Hold on! stan' round thar! no violence—the critter don't know what we mean.

Jackson. Let him answer for the boy, then.

M'Closky. Down with him—lynch him.

Omnes. Lynch him!

[*Exit* LAFOUCHE, R.

Scud. Stan' back, I say I I'll nip the first that lays a finger on Him. Pete, speak to the red-skin.

Pete. Whar's Paul, Wahnotee? What's come ob de child?

Wahnotee. Paul wunce—Paul pangeuk.

Pete. Pangeuk—dead.

Wahnotee. Mort!

M'Closky. And you killed him? [*They approach again.*]

Scud. Hold on!

Pete. Um, Paul reste?

Wahnotee. Hugh vieu. [*Goes* L.] Paul reste el!

Scud. Here, stay! [*Examines the ground.*] The earth has been stirred here lately.

Wahnotee. Weenee Paul. [*Points down, and shows by pantomime how he buried* PAUL.]

Scud. The Injiun means that he buried him there! Stop! here's a bit of leather; [*draws out mail-bags*] the mail-bags that were lost!

[*Sees tomahawk in Wahnotee's belt—draws it out and examines it.*]
Look! here are marks of blood—look thar, red-skin, what's that?

Wahnotee. Paul! [*Makes sign that* PAUL *was killed by a blow on the head.*]

M'Closky. He confesses it; the Indian got drunk, quarreled with him, and killed him.

Re-enter LAFOUCHE, R., *with smashed apparatus.*

Lafouche. Here are evidences of the crime; this rum-bottle half emptied—this photographic apparatus smashed—and there are marks of blood and footsteps around the shed.

M'Closky. What more d'ye want—ain't that proof enough? Lynch him!

Omnes. Lynch him! Lynch him!

Scud. Stan' back, boys! He's an Injiun—fair play.

Jackson. Try him, then—try him on the spot of his crime.

Omnes. Try him! Try him!

Lafouche. Don't let him escape!

Ratts. I'll see to that. [*Draws revolver.*] If he stirs, I'll put a bullet through his skull, mighty quick.

M'Closky. Come, form a court then, choose a jury—we'll fix this varmin.

Enter THIBODEAUX *and* CAILLOU, L.

Thibo. What's the matter?

Lafouche. We've caught this murdering Injiun, and are going to try him. [WAHNOTEE *sits* L., *rolled in blanket.*]

Pete. Poor little Paul—poor little nigger!

Scud. This business goes agin me, Ratts—'tain't right.

Lafouche. We're ready; the jury's impanelled—go ahead—who'll be accuser?

Ratts. M'Closky.

M'Closky. Me?

Ratts. Yes; you was the first to hail Judge Lynch.

M'Closky. [R.] Well, what's the use of argument whar guilt sticks out so plain; the boy and Injiun were alone when last seen.

Scud. (L. C.) Who says that?

M'Closky. Everybody—that is, I heard so.

Scud. Say what you know—not what you heard.

M'Closky. I know then that the boy was killed with that tomahawk—the red-skin owns it—the signs of violence are all round the shed—this apparatus smashed—ain't it plain that in a drunken fit he slew the boy, and when sober concealed the body yonder?

Omnes. That's it—that's it.

Ratts. Who defends the Injiun?

Scud. I will; for it is agin my natur' to b'lieve him guilty; and if he be, this ain't the place, nor you the authority to try him. How are we sure the boy is dead at all? There are no witnesses but a rum bottle and an old machine. Is it on such evidence you'd hang a human being?

Ratts. His own confession.

Scud. I appeal against your usurped authority. This lynch law is a wild and lawless proceeding. Here's a pictur' for a civilized community to afford; yonder, a poor, ignorant savage, and round him a circle of hearts, white with revenge and hate, thirsting for his blood; you call yourselves judges—you ain't—you're a jury of executioners. It is such scenes as these that bring disgrace upon our Western life.

M'Closky. Evidence! Evidence! Give us evidence. We've had talk enough; now for proof.

Omnes. Yes, yes! Proof, proof.

Scud. Where am I to get it? The proof is here, in my heart.

Pete. [*Who has been looking about the camera.*] Top, sar! Top a bit! O, laws-a-mussey, see dis; here's a pictur' I found stickin' in that yar telescope machine, sar! look sar!

Scud. A photographic plate. [*Pete holds lantern up.*] What's this, eh? two forms! The child—'tis he! dead—and above him—Ah! ah! Jacob M'Closky, 'twas you murdered that boy!

M'Closky. Me?

Scud. You! You slew him with that tomahawk; and as you stood over his body with the letter in your hand, you thought that no witness saw the deed, that no eye was on you—but there was, Jacob M'Closky, there was. The eye of the Eternal was on you— the blessed sun in heaven, that, looking down, struck upon this plate the image of the deed. Here you are, in the very attitude of your crime!

M'Closky. 'Tis false!

Scud. 'Tis true! the apparatus can't lie. Look there, jurymen. [*Shows plate to jury.*] Look there. O, you wanted evidence—you called for proof—Heaven has answered and convicted you.

M'Closky. What court of law would receive such evidence? [*Going.*]

Ratts. Stop; this would. You called it yourself; you wanted to make us murder that Injiun; and since we've got our hands in for justice, we'll try it on you. What say ye? shall we have one law for the red-skin and another for the white?

Omnes. Try him! Try him!

Ratts. Who'll be accuser?

Scud. I will! Fellow-citizens, you are convened and assembled here under a higher power than the law. What's the law? When the ship's abroad on the ocean, when the army is before the enemy where in thunder's the law? It is in the hearts of brave men, who can tell right from wrong, and from whom justice can't be bought. So it is here, in the wilds of the West, where our hatred of crime is measured by the speed of our executions—where necessity is law! I say, then, air you honest men? air you true? Put your hands on your naked breasts, and let every man as don't feel a real American heart there, bustin' up with freedom, truth, and right, let that man step out—that's the oath I put to ye—and then say, Darn ye, go it!

Omnes. Go on. Go on.

Scud. No! I won't go on; that man's down. I won't strike him, even with words. Jacob, your accuser is that picter of the crime—let that speak—defend yourself.

M'Closky. [*Draws knife.*] I will, quicker than lightning.

Ratts. Seize him, then! [*They rush on* M'CLOSKY, *and disarm him.*] He can fight though he's a painter; claws all over.

Scud. Stop! Search him, we may find more evidence.

M'Closky. Would you rob me first, and murder me afterwards?

Ratts. [*Searching him.*] That's his programme—here's a pocket-book.

Scud. [*Opens it.*] What's here? Letters! Hello! To "Mrs. Peyton, Terrebonne, Louisiana, United States." Liverpool post mark. Ho! I've got hold of the tail of a rat—come out. [*Reads.*] What's this? A draft for eighty-five thousand dollars, and credit on Palisse and Co., of New Orleans, for the balance. Hi! the rat's out. You killed the boy to steal this letter from the mail-bags—you stole this letter, that the money should not arrive in time to save the Octoroon; had it done so, the lien on the estate would have ceased, and Zoe be free.

Omnes. Lynch him! Lynch him! Down with him!

Scud. Silence in the court; stand back, let the gentlemen of the jury retire, consult, and return their verdict.

Ratts. I'm responsible for the crittur—go on.

Pete. [*To* WAHNOTEE.] See Injiun; look dar [*shows him plate*], see dat innocent: look, dar's de murderer of poor Paul.

Wahnotee. Ugh! [*Examines plate.*]

Pete. Ya!—as he? Closky tue Paul—kill de child with your tomahawk dar; 'twasn't you, no—ole Pete allus say so. Poor Injiun lub our little Paul. [WAHNOTEE *rises and looks at* M'CLOSKY—*he is in his war paint and fully armed.*]

60

Scud. What say ye, gentlemen? Is the prisoner guilty, or is he not guilty?

Omnes. Guilty!

Scud. And what is to be his punishment?

Omnes. Death! [*All advance.*]

Wahnotee. [*Crosses to* M'CLOSKY.] Ugh!

Scud. No, Injiun; we deal out justice here, not revenge. 'Tain't you he has injured, 'tis the white man, whose laws he has offended.

Ratts. Away with him—put him down the aft hatch, till we rig his funeral.

M'Closky. Fifty against one! O! if I had you one by one, alone in the swamp, I'd rip ye all. [*He is borne off in boat, struggling.*]

Scud. Now then to business.

Pete. [*Re-enters from boat.*] O, law, sir, dat debil Closky, he tore hisself from de gen'lam, knock me down, take my light, and trows it on de turpentine barrels, and de shed's all afire! [*Fire seen,* R.]

Jackson. [*Re-entering.*] We are catching fire forward; quick, set free from the shore.

Ratts. All hands aboard there—cut the starn ropes—give her headway!

All. Ay, ay! [*Cry of "fire" heard—Engine bells heard—steam whistle noise.*]

Ratts. Cut all away for'ard—overboard with every bale afire.

*The Steamer moves off—fire kept up—*M'CLOSKY *re-enters,* R., *swimming on.*

M'Closky. Ha! have I fixed ye? Burn! burn! that's right. You thought you had cornered me, did ye? As I swam down, I thought I heard something in the water, as if pursuing me—one of them darned alligators, I suppose—they swarm hereabout—may they crunch every limb of ye!

[*Exit,* L.

WAHNOTE *swims on—finds trail—follows him. The Steamer floats on at back, burning. Tableaux.*

CURTAIN.

END OF ACT FOURTH.

ACT V

SCENE I.—*Negroes' Quarters in* 1.

Enter ZOE, L. 1. E.

Zoe. It wants an hour yet to daylight—here is Pete's hut— [*Knocks.*] He sleeps—no; I see a light.

Dido. [*Enters from hut,* R. F.] Who dat?

Zoe. Hush, aunty! 'Tis I—Zoe.

Dido. Missey Zoe! Why you out in de swamp dis time ob night— you catch de fever sure—you is all wet.

Zoe. Where's Pete?

Dido. He gone down to de landing last night wid Mas'r Scudder; not come back since—kint make it out.

Zoe. Aunty, there is sickness up at the house; I have been up all night beside one who suffers, and I remembered that when I had the fever you gave me a drink, a bitter drink, that made me sleep— do you remember it?

Dido. Didn't I? Dem doctors ain't no 'count; dey don't know nuffin.

Zoe. No; but you, aunty, you are wise—you know every plant, don't you, and what it is good for?

Dido. Dat you drink is fust rate for red fever. Is de folks head bad?

Zoe. Very bad, aunty; and the heart aches worse, so they can get no rest.

Dido. Hold on a bit, I get you de bottle.

[*Exit,* L. R.

Zoe. In a few hours that man, my master, will come for me; he has paid my price, and he only consented to let me remain here this one night, because Mrs. Peyton promised to give me up to him to-day.

Dido. [*Re-enters with phial.*] Here 'tis—now you give one timble-full—dat's nuff.

Zoe. All there is there would kill one, wouldn't it?

Dido. Guess it kill a dozen—nebber try.

Zoe. It's not a painful death, aunty, is it? You told me it produced a long, long sleep.

Dido. Why you tremble so? Why you speak so wild? What you's gwine to do, missey?

Zoe. Give me the drink.

Dido. No. Who dat sick at de house?

Zoe. Give it to me.

Dido. No. You want to hurt yourself. O, Miss Zoe, why you ask ole Dido for dis pizen?

Zoe. Listen to me. I love one who is here, and he loves me— George. I sat outside his door all night—I heard his sighs—his agony—torn from him by my coming fate; and he said, "I'd rather see her dead than his!"

Dido. Dead!

Zoe. He said so—then I rose up, and stole from the house, and ran down to the bayou; but its cold, black, silent stream terrified me— drowning must be so horrible a death. I could not do it. Then, as I knelt there, weeping for courage, a snake rattled beside me. I shrunk from it and fled. Death was there beside me, and I dared not take it. O! I'm afraid to die; yet I am more afraid to live.

Dido. Die!

Zoe. So I came here to you; to you, my own dear nurse; to you, who so often hushed me to sleep when I was a child; who dried my eyes and put your little Zoe to rest. Ah! give me the rest that no master but One can disturb—the sleep from which I shall awake free! You can protect me from that man—do let me die without pain. [*Music.*]

Dido. No, no—life is good for young ting like you.

Zoe. O! good, good nurse: you will, you will.

Dido. No—g'way.

Zoe. Then I shall never leave Terrebonne—the drink, nurse; the drink; that I may never leave my home—my dear, dear home. You will not give me to that man? Your own Zoe, that loves you, aunty, so much, so much.—[*Gets phial.*] Ah! I have it.

Dido. No, missey. O! no—don't.

Zoe. Hush!

[*Runs off,* L. 1. E.

Dido. Here, Solon, Minnie, Grace.

They enter.

All. Was de matter?

Dido. Miss Zoe got de pizen.

[*Exit,* L.

All. O! O!

[*Exeunt,* L.

SCENE II.—*Cane-brake Bayou.—Bank,* C.—*Triangle Fire,* R. C.—*Canoe,* C.—M'CLOSKY *discovered asleep.*

M'Closky. Burn, burn! blaze away! How the flames crack. I'm not guilty; would ye murder me? Cut, cut the rope—I choke—choke!—Ah! [*Wakes.*] Hello! where am I? Why, I was dreaming—curse it! I can never sleep now without dreaming. Hush! I thought I heard the sound of a paddle in the water. All night, as I fled through the cane-brake, I heard footsteps behind me. I lost them in the cedar swamp—again they haunted my path down the bayou, moving as I moved, resting when I rested—hush! there again!— no; it was only the wind over the canes. The sun is rising. I must launch my dug-out, and put for the bay, and in a few hours I shall be safe from pursuit on board of one of the coasting schooners that run from Galveston to Matagorda. In a little time this darned business will blow over, and I can show again. Hark! there's that noise again! If it was the ghost of that murdered boy haunting me! Well—I didn't mean to kill him, did I? Well, then, what has my all-cowardly heart got to skeer me so for? [*Music.*]

[*Gets in canoe and rows off,* L.—WAHNOTEE *paddles canoe on,* R.—*gets out and finds trail—paddles off after him,* L.]

SCENE III.—*Cedar Swamp.*

Enter SCUDDER *and* PETE, L. 1. E.

Scud. Come on, Pete, we shan't reach the house before midday.

Pete. Nebber mind, sar, we bring good news—it won't spile for de keeping.

Scud. Ten miles we've had to walk, because some blamed varmin onhitched our dug-out. I left it last night all safe.

Pete. P'r'aps it floated away itself.

Scud. No; the hitching line was cut with a knife.

Pete. Say, Mas'r Scudder, s'pose we go in round by de quarters and raise de darkies, den dey cum long wid us, and we 'proach dat ole house like Gin'ral Jackson when he took London out dar.

Scud. Hello, Pete, I never heard of that affair.

Pete. I tell you, sar—hush!

Scud. What? [*Music.*]

Pete. Was dat?—a cry out dar in de swamp—dar agin!

Scud. So it is. Something forcing its way through the undergrowth—it comes this way—it's either a bear or a runaway nigger. [*Draws pistol*—M'CLOSKY *rushes on and falls at* SCUDDER'S *feet.*]

Scud. Stand off—what are ye?

Pete. Mas'r Clusky.

M'Closky. Save me—save me! I can go no farther. I heard voices.

Scud. Who's after you?

M'Closky. I don't know, but I feel it's death! In some form, human, or wild beast, or ghost, it has tracked me through the night. I fled; it followed. Hark! there it comes—it comes—don't you hear a footstep on the dry leaves?

Scud. Your crime has driven you mad.

M'Closky. D'ye hear it—nearer—nearer—ah! [WAHNOTEE *rushes on, and at* M'CLOSKY, L. H.]

Scud. The Injiun! by thunder.

Pete. You'se a dead man, Mas'r Clusky—you got to b'lieve dat.

M'Closky. No—no. If I must die, give me up to the law; but save me from the tomahawk. You are a white man; you'll not leave one of your own blood to be butchered by the red-skin?

Scud. Hold on now, Jacob; we've got to figure on that—let us look straight at the thing. Here we are on the selvage of civilization. It ain't our sile, I believe, rightly; but Nature has said that where the white man sets his foot, the red man and the black man shall up sticks and stand around. But what do we pay for that possession? In cash? No—in kind—that is, in protection, forbearance, gentleness; in all them goods that show the critters the difference between the Christian and the savage. Now, what have you done to show them the distinction? for, darn me, if I can find out.

M'Closky. For what I have done, let me be tried.

Scud. You have been tried—honestly tried and convicted. Providence has chosen your executioner. I shan't interfere.

Pete. O, no; Mas'r Scudder, don't leave Mas'r Closky like dat—don't, sa—'tain't what good Christian should do.

Scud. D'ye hear that, Jacob? This old nigger, the grandfather of the boy you murdered, speaks for you—don't that go through you? D'ye feel it? Go on, Pete, you've waked up the Christian here, and the old hoss responds. [*Throws bowie-knife to* M'CLOSKY.] Take that, and defend yourself.

Exit SCUDDER *and* PETE, R. 1. E.—WAHNOTEE *faces him.—Fight—buss.* M'CLOSKY *runs off,* L. 1. E.—WAHNOTE *follows him.—Screams outside.*

SCENE IV.—*Parlor at Terrebonne.*

Enter ZOE, C. [*Music.*]

Zoe. My home, my home! I must see you no more. Those little flowers can live, but I cannot. To-morrow they'll bloom the same—all will be here as now, and I shall be cold. O! my life, my happy life; why has it been so bright?

Enter MRS. PEYTON *and* DORA, C.

Dora. Zoe, where have you been?

Mrs. P. We felt quite uneasy about you.

Zoe. I've been to the negro quarters. I suppose I shall go before long, and I wished to visit all the places, once again, to see the poor people.

Mrs. P. Zoe, dear, I'm glad to see you more calm this morning.

Dora. But how pale she looks, and she trembles so.

Zoe. Do I? [*Enter* GEORGE, C.] Ah! he is here.

Dora. George, here she is!

Zoe. I have come to say good-by, sir; two hard words—so hard, they might break many a heart; mightn't they?

George. O, Zoe! can you smile at this moment?

Zoe. You see how easily I have become reconciled to my fate—so it will be with you. You will not forget poor Zoe! but her image will pass away like a little cloud that obscured your happiness a while—you will love each other; you are both too good not to join your hearts. Brightness will return amongst you. Dora, I once made you weep; those were the only tears I caused any body. Will you forgive me?

69

Dora. Forgive you—[*Kisses her.*]

Zoe. I feel you do, George.

George. Zoe, you are pale. Zoe!—she faints!

Zoe. No; a weakness, that's all—a little water. [DORA *gets water.*] I have a restorative here—will you poor it in the glass? [DORA *attempts to take it.*] No; not you—George. [GEORGE *pours contents of phial in glass.*] Now, give it to me. George, dear George, do you love me?

George. Do you doubt it, Zoe?

Zoe. No! [*Drinks.*]

Dora. Zoe, if all I possess would buy your freedom, I would gladly give it.

Zoe. I am free! I had but one Master on earth, and he has given me my freedom!

Dora. Alas! but the deed that freed you was not lawful.

Zoe. Not lawful—no—but I am going to where there is no law— where there is only justice.

George. Zoe, you are suffering—your lips are white—your cheeks are flushed.

Zoe. I must be going—it is late. Farewell, Dora. [*Retires.*]

Pete. [*Outside,* R.] Whar's Missus—whar's Mas'r George?

George. They come.

Enter SCUDDER.

Scud. Stand around and let me pass—room thar! I feel so big with joy, creation ain't wide enough to hold me. Mrs. Peyton, George Peyton, Terrebonne is yours. It was that rascal M'Closky—but he got rats, I avow—he killed the boy, Paul, to rob this letter from the mail-bags—the letter from Liverpool you know—he sot fire to the shed—that was how the steamboat got burned up.

Mrs. P. What d'ye mean?

Scud. Read—read that. [*Gives letter.*]

George. Explain yourself.

Enter SUNNYSIDE.

Sunny. Is it true?

Scud. Every word of it, Squire. Here, you tell it, since you know it. If I was to try, I'd bust.

Mrs. P. Read, George. Terrebonne is yours.

Enter PETE, DIDO, SOLON, MINNIE, *and* GRACE.

Pete. Whar is she—whar is Miss Zoe?

Scud. What's the matter?

Pete. Don't ax me. Whar's de gal? I say.

Scud. Here she is—Zoe!—water—she faints.

Pete. No—no. 'Tain't no faint—she's a dying, sa; she got pison from old Dido here, this mornin'.

George. Zoe.

Scud. Zoe! is this true?—no, it ain't—darn it, say it ain't. Look here, you're free, you know nary a master to hurt you now: you will stop here as long as you're a mind to, only don't look so.

Dora. Her eyes have changed color.

Pete. Dat's what her soul's gwine to do. It's going up dar, whar dere's no line atween folks.

George. She revives.

Zoe. [*On sofa,* C.] George—where—where—

George. O, Zoe! what have you done?

Zoe. Last night I overheard you weeping in your room, and you said, "I'd rather see her dead than so!"

George. Have I prompted you to this?

Zoe. No; but I loved you so, I could not bear my fate; and then I stood your heart and hers. When I am dead she will not be jealous of your love for me, no laws will stand between us. Lift me; so—[GEORGE *raises her head*]—let me look at you, that your face may be the last I see of this world. O! George, you may without a blush confess your love for the Octoroon! [*Dies.*—GEORGE *lowers her head gently.*—*Kneels.*—*Others form picture.*]

Darken front of house and stage.

[*Light fires.*—*Draw flats and discover* PAUL'S *grave.*—M'CLOSKY *dead on top of it.*—WAHNOTEE *standing triumphantly over him.*]

SLOW CURTAIN

Made in the USA
Monee, IL
03 December 2021

83813117R00046